PAM MUÑOZ RYAN

&

illustrated by
EDWIN FOTHERINGHAM

SCHOLASTIC PRESS • NEW YORK

TOY

BALONEY

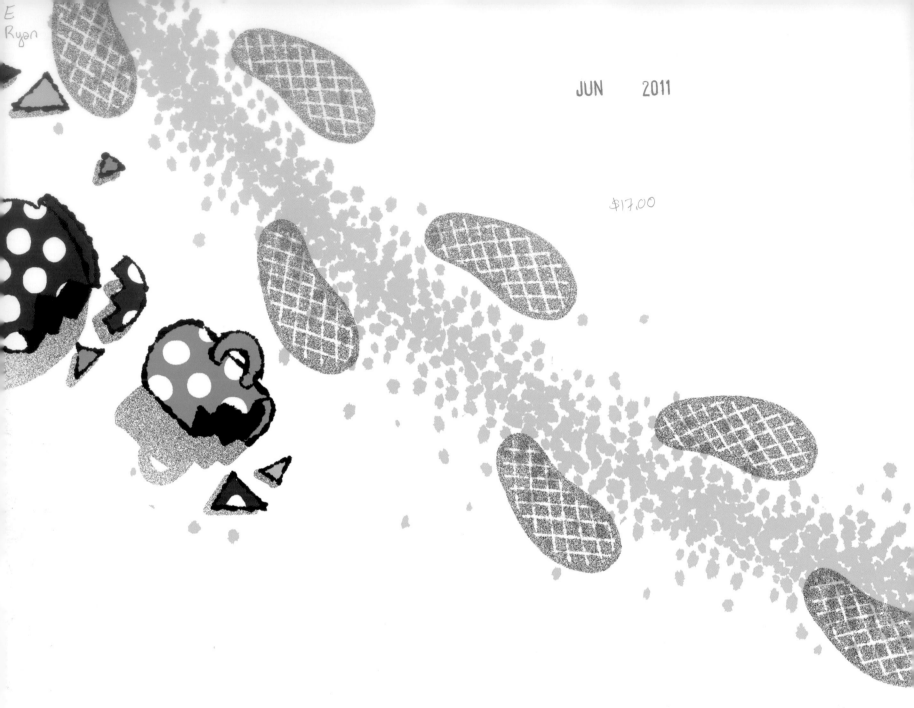

JUN   2011

$17.00

E
Ryan

To Tyler James Ryan —P.M.R.
To Becky, Anna, and Joe. With love —E.F.

Text copyright © 2011 by Pam Muñoz Ryan • Illustrations copyright © 2011 by Edwin Fotheringham • All rights reserved.
Published by Scholastic Press, an imprint of Scholastic Inc., *Publishers since 1920.* • SCHOLASTIC, SCHOLASTIC PRESS, and
associated logos are trademarks and/or registered trademarks of Scholastic Inc. No part of this publication may be
reproduced, stored in a retrieval system, or transmitted in any form or by any means, electronic, mechanical, photocopying,
recording, or otherwise, without written permission of the publisher. For information regarding permission, write to
Scholastic Inc., Attention: Permissions Department, 557 Broadway, New York, NY 10012. • Library of Congress Cataloging-
in-Publication Data Available • ISBN 978-0-545-23135-0 • 12 11 10 9 8 7 6 5 4 3 2 1   11 12 13 14 15 • Printed
in Singapore 46 • The text in this book is set in Stymie BT Medium, Stymie Medium Italic, and Futura Bold. • Illustrations
were done in digital media. • Jacket design by Edwin Fotheringham • Art direction and book design by Marijka Kostiw

Tony Baloney

is a macaroni . . .

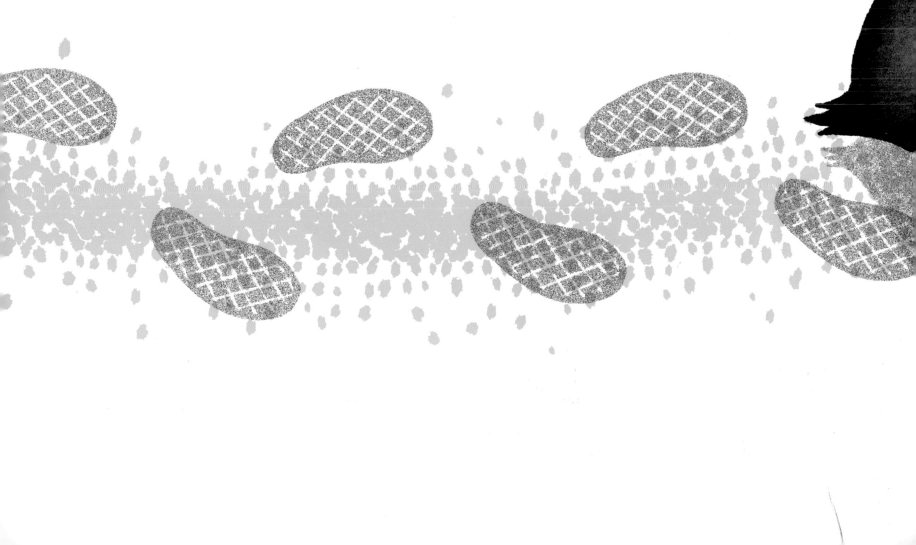

He loves

fish tacos with Parmesan cheese,

Little Green Walrus Guys,

his stuffed animal buddy, Dandelion,

and anything with wheels.

VROOM VROOM

Tony Baloney **does not love** trouble . . .

. . . but trouble **loves** him.

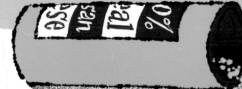

In his family, Tony Baloney is smack
in the middle of the brood.

Dandelion makes sure that Tony Baloney
does not get lost in the crowd.

If he can help it, Tony Baloney stays away

from the Bothersome Babies Baloney

because they are so exasperating!

When it is absolutely necessary, or most of the time, Tony Baloney must play with Big Sister Baloney. He **always** has to be the kitty. "When do I get to be Boss of the World?" asks Tony Baloney.

Big Sister Baloney gives him **the look.**

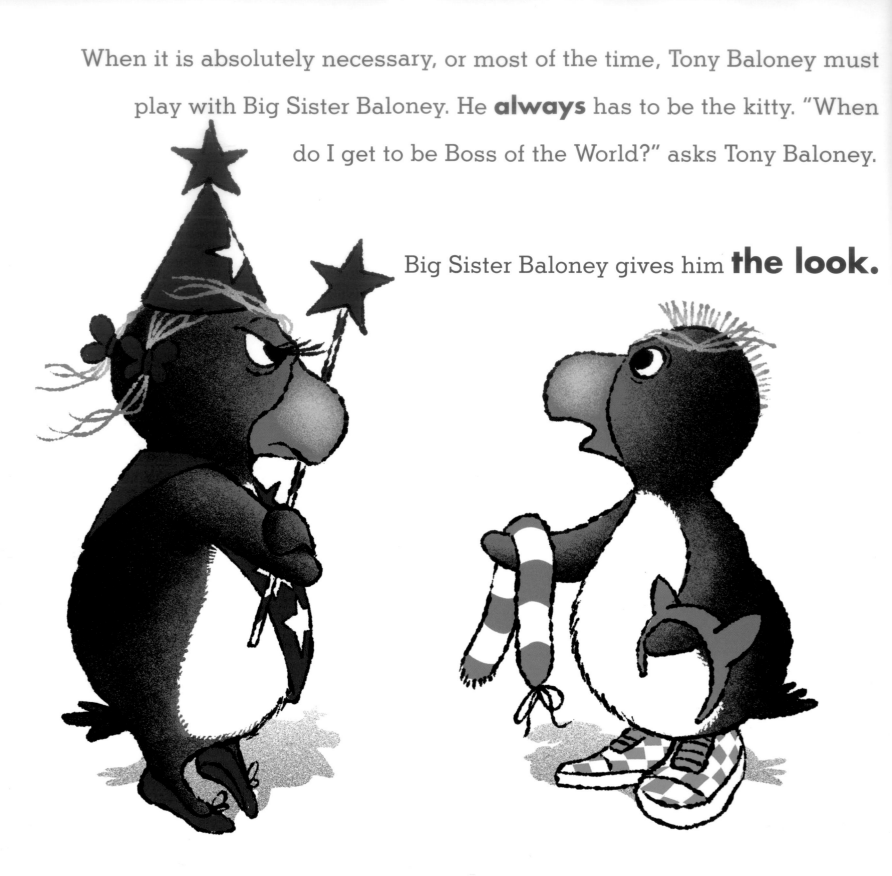

"Meow," says Tony Baloney.

Sometimes, when Tony Baloney is tired of
Big Sister Baloney, and exasperated by
the Bothersome Babies Baloney,
Dandelion behaves badly.

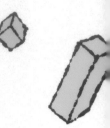

After Dandelion runs amok,

Tony Baloney dashes to his room,

stuffs all of his important things

into his duffel . . .

. . . and makes a fast getaway

to his hidey-space.

Eventually, Momma
and Poppa stop by
for a little chat.

After they leave, Tony Baloney tells Dandelion
all of his woes. As usual, Dandelion is
extremely understanding.

"And then Big Sister said I could not come to her tea party. And the Bothersome Babies chewed off the hands of maybe a hundred, or just one, of my Little Green Walrus Guys. And Momma and Poppa said they love me very much, but I need to think about **our** behavior and using **our** words and saying **we're** sorry.

"Oh, and we have to mean it, too.""

"I guess we should try a little harder to behave," says Tony Baloney.

"I suppose," says Dandelion.

"We have to apologize . . . nicely."

"I am not feeling nicely in my heart."

"How long does it take
for nicely to creep in?"

*"Maybe never, or in a
little while. Just wait for it."*

"You're my very best
buddy in the whole
wide-y world."

*"I know, I know.
Don't get all mushy on me."*

Keep Out

After Tony Baloney has been in the hidey-space for maybe a year, or twenty minutes, he feels a teensy bit lonely, and Dandelion feels a teensy bit like apologizing.

When Tony Baloney
smells fish tacos,
Dandelion feels
even more
like apologizing.

"Dandelion says he's **sorry**."

"I accept Dandelion's apology," Big Sister Baloney huffs, "but what do **you** have to say for yourself, Tony Baloney?"

She gives him **the look.**

Tony Baloney

says nicely,

"I brought Parmesan cheese."

For maybe an hour, or five minutes,

Big Sister Baloney allows

Tony Baloney to be

Boss of the World.

Tony Baloney tells the Bothersome Babies Baloney that **they** must be the kitties.

The babies are surprisingly good at meowing.

"Tony Baloney, you don't ever
have to be the kitty again,"
says Big Sister Baloney.

MEOW

"Never?" says Tony Baloney.

"Never," says Big Sister Baloney.

And she keeps her word.